AWAKE & READY TO DATE

Dating From An Expanded Conscious Perspective

AWAKE & READY TO DATE

Dating From An Expanded Conscious Perspective

BY C. REGI RODGERS

ARPress
ILLUMINATING IDEAS
EMPOWERING VOICES

ARPress
45 Dan Road Suite 5
Canton MA 02021
Hotline: 1(888) 821-0229
Fax: 1(508) 545-7580

Ordering Information:
Quantity sales. Special discounts are available on quantity purchases by corporations, associations, and others. For details, contact the publisher at the address above.

Printed in the United States of America.

ISBN-13:   Paperback   979-8-89389-721-0
           eBook   979-8-89389-722-7

Library of Congress Control Number: 2024922095

CLIENT TESTIMONIALS

"C. Regi Rodgers is a powerful relationship coach. His ability to listen and respond with precise information, never ceases to amaze me. The way he puts together words is an art form in itself. I have talked to him about several relationships and how to navigate my way through them, his advice was kind but direct. I love that his sessions are always a no judgment zone, and I feel free to express myself.

He is a genius at knowing how the human psyche works, in both, male and females.

I will continue to work with him, as long as I have human interaction."
Kym Whitley,
Actor and Comedian

"C. Regi Rodgers, is straight forward when providing relationship expert advice. His guidance tactics, allows you to explore your past experiences so that you are clear on what you want before pursuing a relationship."
CEO Nikki Jennings,
Global Media Group

"C. Regi Rodgers elevates the art of dating to a masterclass in personal growth and connection, crafting a narrative where an expansive mindset fosters profound relationships and lasting love."
Dr. John Wynn,
The Wynn Network

"C. Regi Rodgers is the best when it comes to relationship advice and his power of discernment is second to none. He has this down to a science."
CECE PENISTON
Grammy Nominated R&B Diva

"I truly enjoy working with C. Regi Rodgers on our podcast "THE COACH AND THE COMIC."

His demeanor and calming energy, along with his vast knowledge of relationship information, makes him a reliable relationship COACH and mentor. He has this incredible combination of real life experiences and scientific study with data.

He delivers critical information and insight without malicious rhetoric. He never uses a harsh tone. He listens and gives practical advice as well as wise counsel to those seeking to improve their current relationship. He creates recipes for women and men to guide them on how to attract a mate. It doesn't matter if the relationship is new or old, his recipes are golden.

As a reforming relationship seeker in progress, I know that C. Regi Rodgers will be a source to help me obtain my relationship goals.

He has been the source for so many others to help them with achieving a healthy and wholesome relationship. That's why he's THE COACH and I'm THE COMIC."

BUDDY LEWIS
Actor and Comedian

To determine if you're ready to create a date, consider whether you feel emotionally stable, are you happy with your current life, do you have realistic expectations about dating, and are you open to getting to know someone new; if you're still processing a recent breakup or dealing with significant life stress, it might be best to wait before you awake and become ready to date.

Key questions to ask yourself:

1. *Are you content with your current life?*

2. *Have you adequately processed any recent breakups?*

3. *Do you feel emotionally stable and ready to invest energy in someone else?*

4. *Do you have a clear understanding of what you want in a partner?*

5. *Are you comfortable with your own company and not solely relying on a partner for happiness?*

PREFACE

This book will be all about giving you steps towards learning what "Dating From An Expanded Consciousness" looks and feels like. This all starts in the "mind" (conscious, unconscious, super conscious). You have to recognize the attributes and the function of all your minds. Within each and everyone of our beings we all have strength and courage. There has to be recognition of the quality of strength and courage in your being. Whatever it is that you recognize you energize. Whatever it is that you recognize in your self, you will energize. If you recognize your weakness you will give power to your weakness. If you recognize your faults and your failures you will give power to your faults and your failures. If you recognize your mistakes, you will energize your mistakes.

Be careful what you say about yourself. Don't put yourself down jokingly. Whenever your negative traits come up, do not give them your power of recognition. Don't strengthen your weakness strengthen your strengths. We have a mind inside of us that never forgets anything. You must start recognizing your divine intelligence. Stop reminiscing on your past relationship failures and mistakes and mishaps and wrong choices. You have to accentuate the positive and eliminate the negative, latch on to the affirmative.

Don't ever put yourself down and don't let anyone else put you down. No one can put you down unless you get down on yourself. The only person you have control of in a relationship is you.

You cannot control what someone else does but you certainly can control what you do. If you ever find someone putting you down or getting you down. It's probably because you have put yourself down in one way or another. No one can do you in without your permission.

Don't give energy to your negatives. Where the attention goes the energy flows. As you think so you are.

CHAPTER 1
THE MESSAGE

This message is really all about the science of dating. It is a combination of positive self-image psychology and positive self-motivation. When you believe in yourself positively and correctly, this motivates you to be what you want to be, do what you want to do, and ultimately have what or who you want to have. This message becomes appealing because most of what we have had crammed down our throats in the past hasn't worked in the field of dating. Times have changed, philosophies have changed, so consequently what used to work to some degree, may not work now. Obviously there needed to be some modifications to what we see happening in the field of dating today. Look at our nations divorce rate. There are so many who really don't believe in the sanctity of monogamy and marriage anymore.

This message that I'm sharing with you, positive self-image and positive self-motivation enriches a person and causes you to expand in your consciousness so that you have a awesome and amazing relationship with you first and foremost. If you can get along with you, then you should be able to get along with someone else. If you know how to love you, then you can love someone else. I hope that this book becomes such a driving force in motivating you to take no short cuts when it comes to who you resonate with in your spirit. Relationships can either make you or break you. The challenge is figuring out how to align yourself with someone who resonates with your spirit.

I really want you to comprehend this message and begin to believe in yourself and become positively motivated in regard to what the universe has in store for you. I don't believe and won't approach this book knowing that you will fail in what you want and desire by way of your mate. If you really believe in yourself and do the work that is required, this will work. YOU must work it. Believe in yourself. Believe that you can be and do and have what you desire. Let this book inspire you. The power and the potential that you need to be successful in your quest is in you. If you don't believe in you, this message is not going to work for you. Consciousness is really self-awareness. You should become so aware of YOU and understand YOU. I do realize that people don't like to accept self-responsibility. This message is not about me doing the work for you. This message is about me giving you the tools to do the work for yourself. If you are not being and doing and having what you want. It's something you're doing, stop with the victim mindset and awaken to the victorious expanded consciousness.

This message is about positive self-awareness. Self-awareness is understanding that you don't blame, you take responsibility for whatever is happening in your life. Whatever your self-image is, this becomes gold to you. You have to learn to become the master of your own self-image. You must learn to modify your self-awareness so you can move from self-awareness to self-improvement and then to self-management. This will position you to have what and who you would like to manifest in your life. The strength is within you. When you find this strength and believe in it, then it will motivate you to be and do and have what and who you want to desire. Do you believe in yourself? Everyone has within them the potential to be all they've been designed to be even if it's in love.

CHAPTER 2
THE AWAKENING

It's time to wake up. There's nothing that compares to being awakened and aware. I want to impress upon your sub-conscious mind a positive message and the process that will assist you in receiving the partner that you desire. So many people are unconscious to what lies within them. The present potential that you have within you will be awakened when you realize what power you have within you. When you become awakened to this master mind that is within you, your alliance with your higher self and infinite intelligence will show you the way to manifest the mate that you desire.

It's time to wake up to the presence and power within you that can lead you to the fulfillment of the person or partner that you desire. You have the mind power within you that will enhance your focus and discipline, and in return give you clarity over why you haven't found them yet and why you can't find them. That's because we don't see things as they are, we see things as we are. If you determine to establish a goal and be clear, that empty place or the barren place that's within your mind will not stay void.

This awakening will allow YOU to command your feelings on how to feel. You will always have feelings but you have to take control of your feelings. You don't follow your feelings, you become the master, and your feelings serve and follow you. This is the awakening, "You Are Not Moved By What You See Or What You Feel In The Natural." If you make the above your affirmation continually, this allows your thoughts and your feelings to follow you. Tell your mind what to think. Tell your feelings how to feel and tell your body how to respond. This is the epitome of the awakening. This is called spiritual self-mastery.

The biggest challenge is when we start believing that our mind is us and we identify completely with it. We are not our mind, we are not our behavior, we are not our habits, we are that infinite intelligence that lies behind all that software and all the conditioning.

YOU should be the master of your thoughts. This entails the creation (you) having a oneness with the creator. You ought to master your feelings by telling your feelings how to feel. If you grab a hold of your thoughts, your thoughts will impress upon your feelings. Isn't it a beautiful thing to become awaken and aware? Feelings are thoughts subjectivied on the deepest level. Feeling is the deepest level of thought. When your thoughts reach their deepest level in what the Bible calls the heart and Freud calls the sub-conscious. They reside there as feelings. The things or circumstances that you deal with are in the field of response, and thought is in the field of cause. Which in essence allows you to experience a spiritual euphoria unifying your thoughts with your feelings.

CHAPTER 3
THE PROCESS

What you see is what you get. This is a very mystic statement. This is so true on the psychological level. Whatever you see in your mind in regard to being, doing and having who you desire. You will be led and motivated to take the correct action in order to manifest who you desire. I want you to begin to see yourself manifesting who you desire to have in your life. This can only happen if you are subconsciously conditioned to receive. This is why chapter 1 is so important, because you have to believe in yourself. Do you believe in yourself? You must be committed to yourself and trust the process. The process will allow progress. This is not a one-time application. Repeating this process will allow you to hardwire your brain by introducing new neurotransmitters that will allow you to develop new patterns that will support your manifestations in order to achieve your desired outcome.

The process looks like this:

Step 1 - IMAGINATION - Images or concepts of external objects not present to the senses.

Step 2 - VISUALIZATION- Is a cognitive tool accessing imagination to realize all aspects of an object, action, or outcome.

Step 3 - VIBRATIONAL ALIGNMENT - Every form of matter --your body included vibrates at a certain frequency v i b r a t i o n a l alignment through your emotions with the energy of who you really are. Emotions or e-motions are literally energy in motion.

Step 4 - MANIFESTATION - An event , action, or object that clearly shows or embodies something.

Don't be afraid to step out of your comfort zone and allow life to guide you along your journey. When you trust the process, you accept and have faith in the unknown.

IMAGINATION + VISUALIZATION + VIBRATIONAL ALIGNMENT = MANIFESTATION

Visualization is using your imagination to see yourself manifesting the mate you desire. Why is visualization so powerful? Visualization clarifies what's in your mind concerning who you desire. When you can see your mate in your mind, and you become vibrationally aligned to your desired outcome. This will invite your mate into your physical experience. Visualization clarifies in your mind as to the things you desire. If you don't know what's a fit for you, nor do you know what your mate looks like in a spiritual realm. You probably won't manifest them.

You must learn how to use your mind power to accomplish what you desire in regards to who you desire. Whatever you make clear in your mind, IT MUST HAPPEN. Why? The visualization impresses upon the sub-conscious mind, and the sub-conscious mind takes whatever you input into it and materializes it, then you receive the manifestation by means of what we call sub-conscious correlation and vibratory affinity.

It's important to visualize and use your imagination to see yourself being a manifester. See yourself being happy and full of joy. Know that No one can make you happy unless you know how to make yourself happy. See yourself as a loving person, loving and being loved. I dare you to enter into the secret closet of your soul and shut the door. Shut out doubt and fear and shut out every negative thought. Think of every good reality and be clear on who you want to manifest as your mate. Enter into the theatre of your mind and look upon the stage of your imagination. See and feel what your mate looks like. See in your mind how they walk, talk and all the attributes you want them to have. Remember, No one can make you happy unless you know how to make yourself happy. The Universe is bringing the right person into your life for every right purpose. The Universe is a master choreographer. See yourself in a very happy and successful relationship. See yourself manifesting the mate you desire and the mate you desire manifesting you. See your mate being the ultimate when it comes to being respectful, trustworthy, loving, a good communicator, wise, and someone who has integrity. All that you see in them you feel reciprocated into you.

This process is called mind power. When you learn this process, YOU choose the ideas that you are going to convey to the sub-conscious mind. Give your mind a purpose. A purpose is a goal, it is a direction, a good project. If you give your mind a purpose it will find all of the necessary ways and means of accomplishing the purpose you give it. All you need is the correct positive idea in your mind, it takes ongoing courage and the desire to stay true to the process.

CHAPTER 4

YOU DESERVE THIS

Do you feel your not worthy to have the partner or mate you desire? Do you feel like you are to picky and you will never find them? Have you ever felt like you didn't deserve to have what you want in your mind? There are many who have a great feeling of undeservidness. Where does this feeling come from? Where does this feeling begin? It's not until you get all of these thoughts out of your mind that the magic and manifestation can happen. I'm here to tell you that you deserve to meet the mate of your dreams. Yes you!

In life you get sincerely what you think, feel, and believe you deserve. If you feel like you deserve that new car you get it. If way down in your gut, it's your conviction that your suppose to have it, nothing can keep you from getting it. Allow me to introduce you to REGI'S RELATIONSHIP RECIPE, this philosophy will enhance and empower your feelings of deservedness.

1. Recognition (Visual) - Identification of someone or something or a person from previous encounters. Acknowledgment of something in existence. This brings validity. The perception of something existing or true. Recognize that you deserve this.

2. Realization (Mental) - An act of becoming fully aware of something as a fact. The fulfillment or achievement of something desired or anticipated. This is the state of understanding or becoming aware of something. Realize that you deserve this.

3. Resilience (Emotional) - The capacity to recover quickly from difficulties. This is the ability to spring back into shape,

your elasticity. This gives you the capability to recover after deformation caused especially by compressive stress. With resilience you have the ability to recover from or adjust easily to change. Because of your resilience, you deserve this.

4. Respect (Social) - A feeling of deep admiration for someone or something elicited by their abilities, qualities, or achievements. Respect is a way of treating or thinking about something or someone. This word is also called esteem, it is a positive feeling or action shown towards someone. When you have respect for yourself, you know you deserve everything that comes to you.

5. Readiness (Physical) - The state of being fully prepared for something. The process of readiness involves recognizing the need to change. The condition of being ready. You are ready for action. Be ready for what you deserve.

I want to make a bold statement, "What you feel oftentimes determines what you think you deserve." Isn't it time to change the narrative that you keep saying to yourself? You can't achieve in life more than what you believe in your mind and feel in your heart that you deserve. Within you there is a spiritual subjective intuition that knows instinctively how to position you to get what you deserve from the creator. We tend to ignore it. We put our feelings in a cup and get caught up in a rut. You must feel to the creator (the infinite source within you) like your the one who is entitled to receive what the universe has for you from what you've created in your good thoughts. Do you want to be loved with an honest tongue, feel you deserve it. Do you want to be loved by someone with a devoted heart? Then you must feel you deserve it. Do you want to be loved by someone with exclusive eyes only for you? Then feel you deserve it.

You deserve the mate that you say and believe you deserve. Do you really feel you deserve the mate that you feel you deserve? The Infinite Source is asking you this? Do you feel you deserve what you feel you deserve? I want you to bring yourself to that point that you feel like you are entitled to have the mate of your dreams manifested and tailor made just for you. I want you to know that your spiritual subjective intuitions has and continues to give you instructions and positions you to be in your deserving place. *"The only thing that keeps you from deserving, or loving yourself, or whatever, is someone else's belief or opinion that you have accepted as truth."* Louise Hay

You have to learn how to get way down there in your gut and start learning how to trust your intuition. Master how you feel on a deeper level. Ask yourself, what do you think, what do you feel, what do you believe you deserve. It's time for you to give credence, the mental acceptance to what's true and real. Trust that you deserve the mate you want to attract.

CHAPTER 5
START ATTRACTING WHO YOU WANT

The secret sauce is within you. The term "secret sauce" has come to mean the thing that you do that makes you unique. You must determine what makes you unique. What is the thing in you that would cause someone to be attracted to you. Do you realize that you are a magnet? You can attract a conscious partner. You will become the source to what it means to attract what you want. It's nothing magical it's just understanding how to attract your conscious mate on a spiritual and energetic level. Please note, you have the secret sauce to fulfilling what you desire. You must be deliberate and you must be intentional. This secret sauce can become the power of your imagination. As much as you can see yourself attracting who you desire, you will attract them. As much as you can feel yourself having them, you will have them. Let your imagination expand, this becomes your secret sauce.

Everything begins as a thought that turns into an idea. All of the material things in your life are manufactured out of the ideas of your mind. Developing an original and creative idea requires thinking. We are constantly broadcasting through our thoughts what we are attracting in our physical realm. A manifestation is where your thoughts and your energy can create your reality. The first thing to do when manifesting is to take a look at your thoughts and feelings. If you are constantly being negative, then you are going to attract negative energy. Your personality becomes your personal reality. You are the one who determines and decides who you want to attract in your life. I want you to affirm this. Make this your declaration, say "I am the one who determines and decides who I want to attract into my life." The infinite has given this to you and it is up to you to determine this. According to your acceptance of this belief be it done unto you. How much are you willing to accept. You have the secret sauce inside of you to start attracting, setting your intention sets the tone for the attracting of who you want.

Regi's "SECRET SAUCE" to attraction: REGI's RELATIONSHIP RECIPE:

Step 1 - CLEAN - Do everything possible to clean and unclutter your thoughts so that you can do everything possible to achieve what you desire.

Step 2 - CREATE - Create the vision of what your mate looks like. Bring it into existence.

Step 3 - CHECK - Check your mind to make sure it is filled with positive thoughts related to the vision of how your mate looks. Examine to detect the presence of something.

Step 4 - CONNECT - Bring together or into contact so that a real or notional link is established. Watch your vision become a reality. Start attracting who you want.

CLEAN + CREATE + CHECK = CONNECT (ATTRACT)

Who do you see yourself with? Decide who you want to attract. You must connect with your intention to have them, then you must believe that you will receive what you ask for. Pour all your energy and concentration into seeing it becoming a reality. Everything you want will happen, but it will happen at the right time. You must keep believing. I want you to see, hear, smell, and touch the mate your looking to create. Make it as real as you possibly can, feel them as if you have them already. Add as many details as you can, focus on the end result of attracting who you want. Consider that thoughts are things, and that thinking in a certain way can create concrete changes and attract to you what you desire. Everything that you are ready for is ready for you.

Everyone serves their own individual idea of what they desire. You must be clear, and specific in regards to what you want to attract. There is a consciousness on the individual level and each one of us have our own concept of what we formulate by way of an idea in our mind.

You relate to your own individual concept of what you want to attract. Once again, you determine what you want to attract by CLEANING, CREATING, CHECKING and CONNECTING. When you recognize this secret sauce you then understand this power that you have within you. You can attract to you who you want.

CHAPTER 6

BECOME SELF ACTING

Intentional behavior is when your asking the universe for a mate and it becomes self acting. With this self acting concept, it means you have to break old habit patterns in order for new patterns to form. Self acting doesn't require any external influence or control to function. This is the essential being that distinguishes you from others. This becomes the object of introspection or self action. It's you taking action with intentional behavior. Once again, Intentional behavior is when you become specific when asking the Universe for a mate and it becomes self acting. Let me introduce you to "REGI'S SELF ACTIVATION KEYS" REGI'S RELATIONSHIP RECIPE:

KEY 1# - SELF ACTIVATING - This is having confidence in your own power. (Activating the process)

KEY 2# - SELF MOVING - This means that you are capable of moving independently and confident. (Moving with the flow)

KEY 3# - SELF REGULATING - Taking a pause between your feelings and your actions. (Regulating your emotions)

When you can regulate your emotions this becomes "EMOTIONAL INTELLIGENCE." Emotional intelligence is the capacity to be aware of, control, and express your emotions so that you can communicate effectively, and to handle relationships wisely and empathetically. This gives you the ability to identify and manage your own emotions and actions creating self awareness. Emotional intelligence is essential for long term relationship success. It enables you to become conscious which allows you to stay focused on your priorities. In return you are more mindful and less co- dependent. You increase your emotional awareness and availability so that your "KEYS" activates the process, and allows you to move with the flow, as you regulate your emotions.

All things exist first in and as consciousness. Consciousness in it's simplest form is being aware. Conscious dating must first be sought with clarity, and this comes from within. You have to be clear in order to create your conscious reality. The mental equivalent must be obtained. This equates to becoming self acting. Consciousness is the thought and the feeling of picking a conscious partner that you desire. Consciousness is automatic and self acting. Consciousness is the only thing that acts. You must know the Law Of Consciousness. Understand the State Of Consciousness in which the partner that you desire exist. All things exist in it's correlative state of consciousness. To experience this you must enter into this state of consciousness where your future conscious partner exist.

In an unconscious partnership, you will react without thinking. In your journey for a conscious mate, you will be more intentional in your pursuit. This is why my "3 ACTIVATION KEYS" are so important. I want you to become self-acting and intentional with a natural organic flow attached to it. In a self-acting conscious journey, you understand that the only way you can capture a sense of oneness is to develop the hidden traits that you have within you. In an unconscious pursuit of a mate, your belief is that the only way to have a good relationship is to pick the right partner. In a conscious mind set, you realize you have to become the right partner. Self-acting from an expanded conscious perspective is realizing that *The journey to love isn't about finding the one, it's about becoming the one."* The partner that you desire, you don't seek them first, you first of all establish the thought and the feeling of what you desire. This becomes your thinking, feeling nature. You should establish what you want or desire in your partner in your thinking and feeling nature. When you establish these thoughts and feelings of the mate that you desire within your mind, then it will happen in the natural. Start creating a accurate image of the partner you desire. You become it and it will come to you. This is self-acting from an expanded conscious perspective.

Once you tap into this understanding of consciousness, your thinking shifts into a creative mode and at this point on it's automatic. The mate that you desire is on the way.

CHAPTER 7
THE NEW MIND

Do you realize that how you feel will influence what you think? Your mind is a very powerful thing when you set an intention. When you become conscious in regards to paying attention to your intentions and emotions, whatever it is that isn't working has to go. Albert Einstein said "We cannot solve a our problems with the same thinking we used when we created them." The focused mind pay's attention to its intention. Consciousness is your mind in attention understanding its intention. Having the right mindset means that you understand that your mind must be clear in order to create your conscious reality. Whatever image your mind formulates will replace itself in its physical reality. Expand your awareness of the present moment by feeding your subconscious mind the things you want to see in your life. Be very careful not to feed your sub-conscious mind the things you don't want to see in your life. Don't feed your subconscious mind your bad experiences in your past relationships. Instead feed your subconscious mind new thoughts and ideas about what your next healthy and wholesome relationship looks like. Feed your subconscious mind what love looks like to you. Whatever it is that you put into your subconscious mind, is what you'll get back in return. I want to introduce you to "Regi's 3 Mindsets" REGI'S RELATIONSHIP RECIPE for effective and expanded conscious dating:

1. The Realistic Mindset - This allows you to accept what really is. (Be True to Thyself)

2. The Reasoning Mindset - This requires an eagerness to get things right, even if it means changing your mind. Re-thinking things. (Know Thyself)

3. The Romantic Mindset - This is characterized by the expression of love. (Love Thyself)

Being true to yourself is a personal choice. This means peeling back the layers and being true to what you believe is right and also a fit for you. People have become tired of chasing their heart, because their head and their heart have not been together for a long time. They both have been on two different roads. *"The direction of life is from duality to unity."* Deepak Chopra. There must be a consciousness alignment. When your intellect and emotions are in conflict, this presents a dilemma. When the mate that you create in your mind is in alignment with what you feel in your heart. This becomes a unified wholeness in your energetic field. You must be honest with yourself about what you think, feel, and who you want. Listen to your intuition and trust your inner wisdom. Learn how to wait for what feels right. Learn how to have the feeling of what you want. Do what you know feels right for you. Allow yourself to evolve. Your vibration of the energy of the intention is what attracts.

Knowing thyself means you know what you are capable of accomplishing. This implies that you know who you really are and not who you pretend to be. Always have integrity on how you present yourself through your internal dialogue and your soul expression. How far are you willing to stretch or expand in order to grow in consciousness and love? Again, your mind is a powerful thing when you set your intention. By paying attention to your intention and emotions. This allows you to become more aware of your strengths and weaknesses. Growth in love requires an expansion of consciousness. Growth and consciousness must be in alignment. Be willing to expand your awareness of the present. Have the courage to try new things. Challenge yourself to do what you have never done before in order to get something that you have never received before.

Loving thyself means to have self-respect and a positive self-image and unconditional self-acceptance. Again, whatever image your mind formulates will replace itself in your physical reality. You must love yourself before you can love someone else. It's so important that you are compassionate and empathic and intentional about yourself.

It's a necessary preparation for building a healthy and wholesome relationship with your partner. Identify your good qualities and love those qualities about yourself.

If you feed your subconscious mind with what's not serving your highest good. That's what you will withdraw. What are you putting into your mental screen? What kind of relationship do you see yourself having. Your individual presence of mind should be operated by you and given accurate clear instructions by you. These directives should be given lovingly and consciously. You must tell your mind what you want in your mate, and how you want your mate to function, look, feel, and the specific attributes you want. It is essential that your mind is free and clear, operating from a conscious love. This means to be intentional about the kind of relationship you want to be in. Become deeply committed to growth. How you love yourself is how you teach others to love you.

You are the master of your fate, and you are the captain of your soul. Never let anyone else's thoughts or ideas take up residence in your new mind unless first of all you examine it and choose to have that thought or idea become a part of your new thought rational. You have the power to consciously choose your thoughts and your ideas. Become confident in knowing who you want, do not let anyone else coerce you to think differently. Convince yourself that all you need to do in order to have the mate you desire is be in agreement with yourself. If you can persuade yourself of the reality of having the mate you desire, your mate will come to you. All you have to do is satisfy yourself in your own mind and convey to yourself the reality of your new mind.

CHAPTER 8

LAW OF ATTRACTION

Everything is a condition of the mind. In the New Thought philosophy, the Law of Attraction is the belief that positive or negative thoughts bring positive or negative experiences into a person's life. In the last 7 chapters, my goal was to get you excited about understanding mind conditioning. I want you to expand in the area of consciousness as it relates to dating from an expanded conscious perspective. Your mind must constantly be stretched particularly in the areas where you want the mate you feel you desire and the mate the universe feels you deserve. The Law Of Attraction is the belief that the Universe creates and provides for you that which your thoughts are focused on. Your mind cannot escape conditioning. If you do not consciously condition your mind to have the mate you desire, your friends or other people will condition it negatively. The law of attraction uses the power of the mind to translate whatever is in your thoughts and materialize them into reality. All thoughts turn into things eventually. If you focus on negative you will get negative. If you focus on positive you will get positive. Anything that you can imagine you can achieve. We are human magnets that draw to us what we send out by way of our thoughts and emotions. We attract what we send out.

What matters more than anything is what you say to yourself about yourself. My question to you is, What do you say to yourself about yourself? Whatever you decide in your mind, the universe will produce and allow it to manifest in your life. Because of quantum physics, we have an understanding of the power of the mind and the universe in general. The mind plays a significant role in the shaping of our lives. Each one of us is under the verdict of our own words and choices. Is there someone that you believe is a fit for you and would be a mate that you desire but yet you think you don't deserve them? There is a simple formula, first decide what you want or don't want. Secondly, ask UNIVERSE and be clear on what you want. Our energetic vibrations are like radio signals. Tune your signals to a vibration worthy of receiving it. Thirdly, stay positive and thankful. Oftentimes, you don't receive that person in your life because you can't see yourself with them. I want you to make your mind a blank canvas. Start drawing the pictures of your intended mate on your blank canvas. You are in full control of what you want the picture to look like. If you don't like your first picture, erase it and do another until you come up with one that resonates with your spirit.

"The beginning of love is at the end of resistance" - Danielle Light

Please understand this, you have to open up to expand your consciousness to receive the mate that you truly desire. Once you understand this, everything is within your means. Continue to keep your mind filled with positivity. That takes work, it's something you have to do continuously. It must be done daily. Whatever the subconscious mind listens to, whether it's good, bad or indifferent it believes. If the subconscious mind keeps listening it will believe. I want to give another one of REGI'S RELATIONSHIP RECIPE'S to aid you in the pursuit of another:

REGI'S RELATIONSHIP RECIPE:

1. Be Patient - The capacity to accept or tolerate delay.

2. Be Persistent - Firm or obstinate continuance in a course of action.

3. Don't Be Pushy - Excessive or unpleasant self-assertiveness.

4. Be Polished - Accomplished and skillful.

What role does the Law of Attraction play in your love life? It makes it possible for you to attract your Soulmate/ Twin Flame. The Law is not a respecter of persons. When you see something and you feel it on the inside of you, it's for you. You pick up the vibration from it and you get in tuned or in harmony with the feeling. In other words, it's your spirit that recognizes your encounter that leads to your connection to the mate you desire. Let's look closer at how to manifest the conscious love you desire. You must remove any hinderances or blockages that can prevent you from manifesting the love you desire. When you have been in a bad relationship, you block your heart from believing that love can manifest for you. You cannot go forward if your still holding on to your past. If you have not gotten over your ex this will hinder you from attracting the love you desire.

Who is your mind believing and obeying? The subconscious mind is a believer the conscious mind is the reasoning facet of the mind. If the subconscious receives the same kind of input over and over it will believe what is being inputted. If it keeps hearing the same thing continuously it is going to believe it. If you keep hearing yourself say what your mate looks like, dresses like, and feels like. If you continue to keep your mind filled with positivity, you will begin to believe it and you will have the encounter you desire and the mate the Universe knows you deserve. When you truly want something and believe for it without limiting yourself with disbelief, the universe will make it happen.

CHAPTER 9

YOUR TWIN FLAME

A Twin Flame is when two people are perfectly matched. The important part of this encounter is in the dynamic between the two people, and it's where you understand the difference between a twin flame and a life partner or soulmate. I tell people so often that I'm not looking for my soulmate, I'm looking for my twin flame, and I expect her to be ready for me when I find her. If you are favored in this life to find your Twin Flame, the two of you will be pulled together like magnets. When you encounter the person who carries the other half of your energy, it can create a profound and life altering sense of wholeness. What is a Twin Flame? It's the other half of your soul. It's your mirror. If you compare a Twin Flame vs. Soulmate you will discover that a Soulmate is someone who is made from the same kind of energy as you, but who has never existed in fusion with you. An encounter with a Twin Flame is on another level.

Why do we use mirrors? Mirrors are objects that reflect light in a way that is most proportionate to the original object. As a mirror, a Twin Flame reflects back to you your weaknesses but also your greatest strengths. Usually their presence brings on a lot of personal growth and transformation. A Twin Flame elevates your self knowledge, including knowledge of your flaws. Twin Flames are sometimes referred to as Twin Souls. *We think we meet someone with our eyes. But we actually meet them with our soul* - Mimi Novic. Twin Flames are called this because they are thought to be two parts of a soul that split and incarnate into Earth so that they can learn and grow. The diverse experiences they gather when they are away from each other help to create their separate identities as souls. When the two reunite, they form the ultimate relationship. All other relationships before this one serve as practice for this ultimate one. Meeting a Twin Flame is a special, life-altering moment. When you have an encounter with your Twin Flame, this will jumpstart a new part of your life. It will facilitate growth, inspire change and challenge you to fully accept yourself.

It seems that once you've reached a certain level of consciousness in life, your soul splits in two before settling into your physical self. Basically, this means that the two of you are wandering planet earth. The other you is your twin flame and when you have that encounter, you immediately feel as if you're whole again. The purpose of the prior chapters were to get you in an energetic space so that you would become awakened to doing the inner work so that you can experience this and have the mate you desire and that mate that desires you. Relationships can offer incredible radical personal growth. Relationships can either make you or break you. The challenge is finding someone who resonates with your spirit. Relationships can offer incredible radical personal growth as powerful as any spiritual practice. And there's no better example to look at this than in a twin flame relationship.

The real purpose of a Twin Flame is not about great sex, emotional highs and an epic love story. It's purpose is to wake you up, shake you up and call you higher. It's a gift presented by the divine. They will mirror back to you everything in your life that you need to address.

Everything that has not been healed. They come into your life to show you YOU. The amount of energy created when you are together is magnetic. People around you will notice and feel the power between you. When you find your Twin Flame, the two of you can become an unstoppable force. You will feel an immediate bond or connection through this encounter. It will feel like you've known them before and their energy feels very familiar. The two of you will feel each other even when you are apart. There seems to be a hard time getting each other out of each other's mind. It could feel like an obsession but it's not. The two of you are so closely CONNECTED that you literally feel each other. I want to show you "REGI'S ROAD" REGI'S RELATIONSHIP RECIPE to understanding the Twin Flame Process:

REGI'S ROAD:

- LOOKING ROAD - Two souls are wondering planet earth in search for one another.

- ALERT ROAD- Being in an energetic space that allows for the awakening.

- TRIAL ROAD - Accepting the challenge to fully accept yourself.

- EMERGENCY ROAD - There's the potential for conflict.

- CONCEDE ROAD - The two are so connected that they literally feel each other.

- REJOINING ROAD - When the two reunite, the ultimate relationship is formed.

"People take different roads seeking fulfillment and happiness. Just because they're not on your road doesn't mean they've gotten lost." Dalai Lama.

The road to finding your Twin Flame may vary for different people. There is one infusing factor that you will be able to certainly appreciate. A road to finding them does exist. Therefore it is important that you respect the road that others take and accept the road that you've taken. Be open minded and clear ready to accept and acknowledge that your Twin flame is locating the road to travel for the two of you to have a everlasting encounter.

CHAPTER 10
DECIDE WHAT YOU WANT

Getting to a place where you decide what you want and who you want to select as your mate is important. You must know what is a fit for you. Are you ready for your Twin Flame? Are you ready for the person who's going to love you in spirit? Speak to the Universe and put it into the atmosphere. Be very specific and clear as it relates to who and what your mate looks and feels like.

You have the ability which equates to power to command and speak into existence who you would like to have as your mate. You must become excited about what you want. Make a decision and feel enthused about it. You should become excited and delighted. If who you want as a mate doesn't stimulate your senses and get's you feeling elated, then you probably have the wrong mate to want.

Write down on a piece of paper what your mate looks like. Be very detailed on the attributes that you would like them to have. Ask yourself the question, what does my mate/ partner look like and what is a fit for me? I want you to be able to identify this individual when the universe allows your paths to cross or when you have an encounter with them. As you write these things down if your not enthused, then you need to start over until you feel exhilarated about what you are writing. I need you to be extremely ignited about what your decision is. Arrive at a place in your mind that happiness is you and you are happy with your decision. Become more real, authentic, passionate, happy and present. This makes you more beautiful and attractive to the person that you will create. Get rid of whatever dogma's or beliefs that may be holding you back. There are lot's of hidden beliefs that will hinder you from making a decision in regards to what you want. Let's not focus on what's missing such as, your not good enough for anyone, there's no good one's left, you'll never meet the right person….etc. These beliefs limit the power of intention and prohibits your confidence in making a decision about what you want. Whatever you give attention to is what will expand. Let me give you another REGI'S RELATIONSHIP RECIPE to assist you with your decision "On How To Decide What You Want."

1. JUST BE YOURSELF- Tap into what feels right for you. This isn't about what others are telling you need. Know for yourself.

2. DEVELOP THE QUALITIES YOU WANT IN SOMEONE ELSE IN YOURSELF- Become what you want. Possess the character traits that you desire.

3. LIVE YOUR LIFE MORE FULLY- Learn to accept and love yourself more fully. This in return will allow you to be loved more fully.

What is your attitude towards who you want in your life as your mate/partner? Attitude is said to define the personality of a person. Your attitude has everything to do with you deciding who you want. Your attitude has everything to do with the experience or encounter that you will have with your mate. According to Winston Churchill, attitude is a small thing that makes a big difference. What if you determine that you are truly an amazing person? What if you decide in your mind that there are so many wonderful individuals out there waiting just for you? Having this type of attitude will give you the confidence to carry yourself in a manner that becomes attractive to others. The power of belief and intention is enormous. Your attitude will have all to do with how the encounter and when the encounter will happen. Your attitude will decipher whether or not you meeting your Twin Flame will ever happen. Make a decision and determine in your mind that you are going to be happy and excited about deciding what you feel you deserve. Here are the 5 ingredients to having the right attitude:

REGI'S "RELATIONSHIP ATTITUDE:"

1. Optimistic Attitude - This is a belief that the outcome will be positive, favorable or desirable.

2. Expectation Attitude - This is the belief that what your expecting will occur.

3. Enthusiastic Attitude - This means you get satisfaction in getting things done and pursuing what you like.

4. Confident Attitude - This means you accept and trust yourself. You have a positive view of your qualities.

5. Cheerful Attitude - This means you surround any situation and the people you have an encounter with cheer and being positive.

Everything begins in the mind and you being in agreement with yourself creates a vibration. You must be in tuned with the infinite. Ask yourself this question, do you have a repulsive attitude towards who you say you want as your mate? There is a certain mentality that you must possess. Strategic thinking involves making a series of decisions in regards to what your intentions are. All of the above "Relationship Attitude's" play a major role in strategic thinking. Strategic thinking enables you to take the most logical approach with a expanded conscious perspective in order to receive the best results. You have to engage with the process. You cannot be indifferent with yourself and then expect you to have what you say you want as it relates to your mate. When you meet someone that you have a good connection with, make room so that the connection can develop and grow. Don't be indifferent when it comes to what you decide is a fit for you. This type of thinking will create problems that you don't think has anything to do with your attitude. Get to a place of peace and wholeness with yourself. This becomes a place of agreement and solidarity about what you decide you want. Make a choice that allows you to determine who will be a fit for you based on your qualities. Write a list of qualities that you believe are a fit for you. Separate the list into 3 categories: Articulate your standards clearly.

1. Dealmakers - The qualities that are absolutes for you.

2. Deal breakers - The qualities that typically don't work for you.

3. Non-negotiables - The qualities that are absolutely not for you.

There are many thoughts and feelings to process, and many questions to be asked as you are deciding what you want. Ask yourself this question, *"is what you want going to be for your highest good?"* *"Discipline is remembering what you want."* - David Campbell. Stay focused, don't ever lose hope, and always exude good energy. Focus your attention on choices that align with what you want.

CHAPTER 11
YOUR TRANSFORMATION

Transformation is the process of changing. Oftentimes the change that takes place is for the better. Transformation is profound. Transformational change is both radical and sustainable. The whole purpose of transformation is to transform you so that you don't go back to what you were. There is a Cosmic Law that says, "Whatever it is that you are indifferent towards, it will also be indifferent towards you." You must be conscious of the application of the laws.

The process of transformation is a process that produces significant improvement in performance. I want to give you REGI'S RELATIONSHIP RECIPE FOR TRANSFORMATION:

1. EXPANDING - This is the simplest to transform. It expands what your currently doing rather than creating something new. It improves what already exist.

2. EVOLUTIONARY - This replaces what already is with something completely new. You must dismantle and emotionally let go of the old way of operating while the new way is being installed.

3. EXPERIMENTAL - This is much more challenging for 2 distinct reasons. First, the future state is unknown when you begin and is determined through trial and error as new information is gathered. Second, there must be a radical change with new a mindset and behavior. The actual transformation process must emerge as you go.

Transformation can be very impactful. There has to be an inner shift of the mindset. This can require an external implementation of new processes and a different modus operandi. You should start now by creating the pictures in your mind, design a vision board and establish the mate you want and desire and the mate that the universe knows you deserve. What do they look like? Utilize the standards that I taught in the last chapter. These scientific techniques work. There are no excuses for anyone reading this book. You should begin making the preparations to institute pictures on your board representing the mate you desire, and the relationship you want. It is so important that you understand the principles that you have received in the previous chapters. I hold you accountable for being conscious, awakened, and aware.

May I suggest to you that you get some magazines and photographs that represent the mate and relationship you desire. I want you to become the architect of what your outer and inner eyes behold. If your eyes both your inner and outer are always gazing upon negative relationships, divorces, breakups, cheating...etc., this is what you will become and create in your space. What you see outward is really controlled by what you see inward. I want to get you to a place that you become ultra conscious of this.

What you see with your inner eye truly has the power to nullify that which is in the outward. I want you to now start displacing the negative and replacing it with the positive. Can you affirm this with me? Make this affirmation "I am now displacing the negative and replacing it with the positive." You really need to see yourself outside yourself.

In a movie theatre, the film in the projector is greater than the image on the screen. If you want to change the image on the screen you have to go to the projector and change the film. What is the film? It's the thought. It becomes even deeper than this. Let's look at the actors and actresses who've performed for the production of the film. You are the actors and actresses that make and project your film. You are the producer and this knowledge and information gives you power.

Once you know that the reality is not on the screen, and that you have the power to change the film, this allows you to be transformed. If you don't like the drama filled film that's playing on the screen, take out the drama filled film and put in a romantic love story. Stop sitting there crying because of the drama when you have the ability to transform and do something about it.

The more you think about the negatives in regards to relationships. The more you will create this in your world of experiences and encounters with your potential mate. You have the power to overcome this. Become transformed by the renewing of your mind. This word transform is the Greek word for metamorphosis. This word metamorphosis comes with the understanding that it is the process of transformation from an immature form to an adult form in two or more distinct stages. It also means a change of form or nature of a thing or person into a completely different one, by natural or supernatural means.

Let's explore a butterfly's life cycle in detail concentrating on three out of the four stages of it's life. All butterflies have a complete metamorphosis. To grow into an adult they go through 4 stages. Each stage of transformation has a different goal. Let's look at 3 of these stages and see what we can learn.

The Caterpillar Stage which follows right after hatching from the egg which is the first stage. The main task in the caterpillar stage is consumption. The caterpillar's purpose is to eat as much as possible in order to fuel the growth that will take place in the future. During this stage the caterpillar will outgrow and shed it's skin as many as four or five times. This should represent the learning stage for you. This book has given you some principles that may have made you feel uncomfortable especially about dating from an expanded conscious perspective. There will be some shedding of your old thoughts and ideas about dating. During this stage you will begin to discover what is a fit for you and what isn't a fit for you as is relates to your mate. This should be a stage of excitement and good energy because of your flow of energy. What consumes your mind will control your life. You should find yourself moving to a good energetic space.

The Chrysalis Stage is the most intriguing stage of a butterfly's development. When this crawler is fully grown and can eat no more, it simply dangles from a branch and spins a protective cocoon around itself so that it can safely rest and digest all the food that has been consumed in the previous stage. Though the chrysalis appears unchanged from the outside during this stage, there is a dramatic transformation taking place on the inside. This should represent the stage now where you are in the process of growing from all of the principles and laws that you've learned through the chapters so that you can transform into something new, and your perspective has become expanded. Push through this stage, push forward and understand you have the power, and the power is within you. Push forward and don't let anyone tell you anything different.

The Butterfly Stage is the last and final stage. The fully developed butterfly is ready to emerge from the Chrysalis stage. After breaking free, the butterfly's wings are still folded and wet and more rest time is necessary to allow blood to flow into the wings. When the wings are fully dry, the butterfly is ready to take flight and share it's beauty with the world. During this stage you move with intent. There is attention with intent to break free. In this stage you have created your vision board and you are very clear and specific about what your mate looks and feels like. You know what you desire and what the universe knows you deserve. Your actions are in alignment with your words, there is a oneness and a spirit of peace. You are ready to display your new growth to the world. You are going to leave behind the old way of thinking and what you thought about relationships and dating. You are now ready to embrace this philosophy of "Dating From An Expanded Conscious Perspective."

CHAPTER 12

DATING FROM AN EXPANDED CONSCIOUS PERSPECTIVE

If we are what we think about, then we have to be very careful what we think about. This means it's imperative that we are very cautious yet conscious of every conversation that we have with whomever that focuses on what's MISSING. Through the assistance of this book, I hope you are becoming more aware of what you do, what you experience, how you react, and what your reaction actually shows you. "We are what we repeatedly do. Excellence then is not an act, but a habit." - Aristotle

Working on expanding your consciousness gives you the ability to dream and increases your experiences beyond your imagination.

If you really want to attract someone into your life and your still continuously talking about what's missing, there has to be an understanding that what you think and talk about is what EXPANDS. There will be a continued expansion of what's missing and you will continue to attract what's missing. EXPANDED CONSCIOUSNESS is having an understanding to not talk about what's MISSING (not having a partner, boyfriend, girlfriend, wife, husband, fiancé). With EXPANDED CONSCIOUSNESS it's about putting your attention on what you intend to create. It's having the attention with the purpose on intention.

Be sure to have substance when it comes to focusing on what is important to you. Many of the concepts and "Regi's Relationship Recipes" that I have shared with you are to get you to a place of understanding your core values. Core values are your fundamental beliefs in order to make you feel safe, protected and connected. Relationship core values are principles that dictate your behavior, your personal perspective, not just about yourself but also your future partner. You must know what you value in your relationship. I'm sure you've organically and naturally developed your own unique set of core values. Don't ever compromise. If someone's values don't align with yours, then they probably are not a fit. Your core values are so intrinsic to who you are. This is why you become better suited to a partner who shares your values and beliefs. If you are not aware of what your core values are, it will become very difficult for you to recognize a partner with whom you are fundamentally compatible with. I want you to expand in your consciousness and ask yourself these questions. How important is honesty, accountability, trust, communication, loyalty, religion, self-discipline, self-improvement, integrity, growth? Your answers to each of the above will aid you in figuring out what you value most. You may even want to add to the list. List each item from most important to least important. This helps to expand your consciousness, and not focus on what's missing but having a better understanding of what you intend to create.

I want you start looking beyond what the outer eye sees and you grab a hold to what the inner eye knows. You may not have a boyfriend or girlfriend, but your conversation is, he or she is on the way. Whoever you want to attract in your life you must know that they are on the way. In order for you to understand dating from an expanded conscious perspective, you must be in alignment with yourself.

This is all about getting your thoughts in harmony with the source. When this happens you begin to ELEVATE AND EXPAND your thoughts so that they become more harmonized with what and who you want to attract. This has to become a natural way of how you think on a continuous basis.

When you shift into an EXPANDED CONSCIOUSNESS PERSPECTIVE, this creates an anticipation that you will have what you desire and what the universe knows you deserve. It has been said that anticipation becomes your breeding ground for your miracle. As you transform into deeper consciousness and your thoughts become higher, they begin to EXPAND. You become more and more in line with what you want to attract. This is the epitome of EXPANDED CONSCIOUSNESS FROM A DATING PERSPECTIVE. The Universe, God, Source, Source Energy call it what you want, but it starts to conspire with you because you are now in harmony with it.

When we become in harmony we become a collaborator with fate. And instead of fate being something that might or might not happen to you, you are now in collaboration with what it is that you want to happen.

Don't put your thoughts on what's missing. Don't put your thoughts on what's always been. Don't put your thoughts on what others want for you. Don't put your thoughts on any other thoughts that are out of harmony than the relationship that you would like to have for yourself. You know what you desire and the Universe knows what you deserve. You must condition your mind powers for what you desire and want. You will receive whatever it is you condition your mind to receive. If you feel like you can be your authentic self when in the presence of a potential partner without sacrificing or compromising any of your core values, you are probably on your way to a healthy, happy, expanded conscious relationship.

"REGI'S RELATIONSHIP RECIPE" FOR EXPANDED CONSCIOUS DATING:

1. BE READY

2. RECOGNIZE

3. RECEIVE

DATING FORM AN EXPANDED CONSCIOUS PERSPECTIVE QUESTIONS

I want you to explore your past relationships and experiences around love. The intent is to get you to connect with your spirit. This becomes the tool to unveil your deepest heart's desire and gain an incredible amount of insight and clarity for dating and relationships moving forward. It is highly recommended that you set aside a time of day, each day to read, meditate and focus on what you plan to create. Do your best to give yourself at least a half hour, but if you really want to get the most out of it, commit an hour in the morning and or the evening to dig deep into the inner sanctum of yourself.

Invite in the energy of love to this process. Take yourself on a date to find and gift yourself the perfect journal that is reflective of love and relationship for you. As you embark on this, set an intention that speaks to your commitment to your personal growth in love and relationships.

Some examples of intentions are:

1. I intend to be fully engaged open to challenging my beliefs about love.

2. I choose to be more open and available for receiving love in my life.

With this focus, the journey will have even more meaning for you personally and it will have a greater impact on your life.

Stay Connected with me on Facebook, share your experiences along the way! There are women across the globe who are experiencing Dating From An Expanded Conscious Perspective with you!

www.facebook.com/C Regi Rodgers

If you've enjoyed the book tell your friends to order their copy NOW!
www.cregirodgers.com

Chapter 1
The Message

When you believe in yourself positively and correctly, this motivates you to be what you want to be, do what you want to do, and ultimately have what or who you want to have.

1. Think back to the first time you felt attracted to someone, who was that person?

____

2. Did you let them know what you were feeling?

____

3. What did that feeling make you think about yourself?

____

4. Did you believe that this was a normal feeling or were you amazed because you felt something you had never felt before?

____

ASSIGNMENT:

Write down how you harnessed your feelings the first time you reacted to what you felt.

____

____

____

____

____

Chapter 2
The Awakening

It's time to wake up. There's nothing that compares to being awakened and aware. I want to impress upon your sub-conscious mind a positive message and the process that will assist you in receiving the partner that you desire.

1. Think back on when you had that first lustful feeling, what type of individual where you attracted to?

____

2. Did that person mold what attracts you today?

____

3. Was there a rhythm that was developed that put you on a course that says, you like a certain type of person?

____

4. What type of individual do you believe you are because of that experience?

____

ASSIGNMENT:

Write down what you feel are the characteristic traits of someone that you think turns on your lust meter on.

____

____

____

____

____

Chapter 3
The Process

The process will allow the progress. This is not a one-time application. Repeating this process will allow you to hardwire your brain by introducing new neurotransmitters that will allow you to develop new patterns that will support your manifestations in order to achieve your desired outcome.

1. When you hear the word imagination what type of mate do you imagine?

____

2. Are you comfortable enough in your skin to say what turns you on?

____

3. If you are with someone, will you tell them what's on your mind or do you keep them guessing?

____

4. When you hear the word visualization, are you able to imagine and feel how you want your relationship to look like?

____

ASSIGNMENT:

Write down the feelings that you get when you see someone that you desire.

____

____

____

____

Chapter 4
You Deserve This

I'm here to tell you that you deserve to meet the mate of your dreams.

1. Do you feel like you have compromised up until this point?

____

2. What does the word "compromise" mean to you?

____

3. Why do you think that you have settled in the past for what doesn't make you thoroughly happy?

____

4. Have you ever felt like you didn't deserve to have what you want in your mind?

____

ASSIGNMENT:

Describe the feeling you get when you desire to be with someone?

Write down how the feeling makes you feel.

____
____
____
____
____

Chapter 5
Start Attracting Who You Want

It's nothing magical it's just understanding how to attract your conscious mate on a spiritual and energetic level.

1. What is your secret sauce?

____

2. What is the thing in you that would cause someone to be attracted to you?

____

3. What makes you a magnet?

____

4. What steps are you taking to be more positive?

____

ASSIGNMENT:

Write down what you feel is stopping you from being the fearless individual you need to be so that you could attract the one you want.

____

____

____

____

____

Chapter 6
Become Self Acting

Self acting doesn't require any external influence or control to function. This is the essential being that distinguishes you from others.

1. Do you think you are insecure?

____

2. If yes, what areas would you say you have insecurities?

____

3. Do you believe you can stand on your own or do you feel like you must have someone in your life to validate your self-worth and worthiness?

____

4. What does the word "validation" mean to you? How do you apply this word in an encounter with someone?

____

ASSIGNMENT:

Write down Regi's Self Activation keys and list in detail how each one will assist you in your relationship encounters.

____

____

____

____

____

Chapter 7
The New Mind

Having the right mindset means that you understand that your mind must be clear in order to create your conscious reality.

1. Knowing yourself means you know what you are capable of accomplishing. What do you feel you have accomplished?

____

2. Being true to thyself is a personal choice, are you being true to yourself?

____

3. Loving thyself means to have self-respect and a positive self-image and unconditional self-acceptance. Do you have these attributes?

____

4. Do you trust your inner wisdom?

ASSIGNMENT:

Write down which one of "REGI'S 3 MINDSETS" is more true to your very quiescence. Once you discover which one represents you. Start applying this into the journey of your new beginning.

____
____
____
____

Find the courage and strength to move out of fear, doubt and resistance and into something new. Are you ready to live your new results?

Chapter 8
Law Of Attraction

The Law of Attraction is the belief that positive or negative thoughts bring positive or negative experiences into a person's life.

1. If you focus on positive you will get positive, do you have a positive mindset?

   ____

2. We attract what we send out, what are you attracting?

   ____

3. Are you blocking your heart from believing that love can manifest for you?

   ____

4. How is the Law Of Attraction influencing your love life?

   ____

ASSIGNMENT:

One of REGI'S RELATIONSHIP RECIPE'S is "Be Polished." What does this mean to you?

____

____

____

____

____

Chapter 9
Your Twin Flame

A Twin Flame is when two people are perfectly matched.

1. What is a twin flame?

____

2. What's the difference between a twin flame and a soul mate?

____

3. Do you think you have ever met your twin flame?

____

4. Has there been anyone that you've had trouble getting out of your mind?

____

ASSIGNMENT:

According to REGI'S 6 ROAD's recipe which road resonates most with you? Why and how?

____

____

____

____

Chapter 10
Decide What You Want

Getting to a place where you decide what you want and who you want to select as your mate is important.

1. Are you ready for your twin flame?

____

2. Do you have a repulsive attitude towards who you say you want as your mate?

____

3. Are you clear and specific about who you want in your life?

____

4. Are you ready to make a decision?

____

ASSIGNMENT:

Write down what are your deal- makers, deal-breakers and non-negotiables.

____
____
____
____

Bonus Question: Which one of REGI'S RELATIONSHIP ATTITUDES sums you up the best?

____
____

Chapter 11
Your Transformation

Transformation is the process of changing.

1. When you see yourself outside yourself what do you see?

____

2. What does transformation mean to you?

____

3. Have you had the tendency to gaze upon negative relationships in the past?

____

4. What's the purpose of transformation?

____

ASSIGNMENT:

Create a vision board and establish the mate you want and desire and the mate the universe knows you deserve. What do they look like? Start by creating the pictures in your mind.

____

____

____

____

____

Chapter 12
Dating From An Expanded Conscious Perspective

When you shift into an EXPANDED CONSCIOUSNESS PERSPECTIVE, this creates an anticipation that you will have what you desire and what the universe knows you deserve.

Expanded Consciousness is having the ability to not talk about what's missing. How important is Expanded Consciousness to your thought process.

____

Do you feel it's important to condition your mind powers to what you desire and want?

____

What are you planning on creating?

____

Do you shrink back when your aware that your feelings of LOVE are more than the other?

____

ASSIGNMENT:

Write down what you feel the difference is between LIKE, LOVE and IN LOVE then write down THE WAY YOU FEEL when you LIKE someone, LOVE someone and IN LOVE with someone.

____

____

____

____

What habits must you adopt to achieve the results you want?

____

____

____

____

____